The TRANSFORMERS™ — Robots in Disguise!

They came from Cybertron—a planet of machines—where war raged for thousands of years between the noble Autobots and the evil Decepticons.

NOW THE BATTLE OF THESE POWERFUL ROBOTS IS YOUR BATTLE!

ONLY YOU can protect the earth from the evil destruction of the Decepticons!

Read the directions at the bottom of each page. Then decide what the Autobots should do next.

If you decide correctly, the Autobots will triumph! If you make the wrong choices, the unspeakable evil of the Decepticons will rule the world!

Hurry! T[...]ge 1.

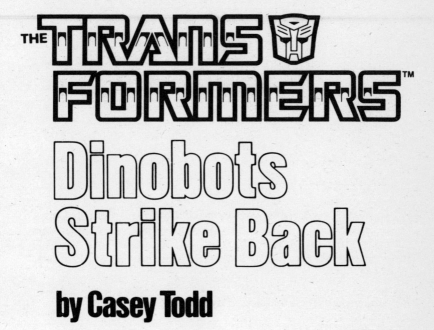

THE TRANSFORMERS™

Dinobots Strike Back

by Casey Todd

BALLANTINE BOOKS • NEW YORK

Library of Congress Catalog Card Number: 85-90606

ISBN: 0-345-32669-5

Editorial Services by Parachute Press, Inc.

Illustrated by William Schmidt

Designed by Gene Siegel

Manufactured in the United States of America

First Edition: December 1985

10 9 8 7 6 5 4 3

Dinobots
Strike Back

Kaboom!!! The mortar explodes at their feet, knocking down Grimlock, Slag, Snarl, and Sludge. Only Swoop sees the bomb coming, seconds before it explodes. He transforms into his pterodactyl form and tries to fly to safety in a nearby tree. Although he escapes, the bomb injures one of his powerful wings.

Swoop watches in horror as Bombshell transforms into his tiny insect form and starts to attack the other Dinobots. Bombshell uses his stinger to inject cerebro-shells into the heads of the unconscious Dinobots. Now he can control the minds of his victims.

Bombshell turns back into his robot form and orders Kickback to report back to Megatron. "Tell our great leader that I, Bombshell, have complete control over the Dinobots."

"Megatron will reward us well for this," says Kickback as he leaves for Decepticon headquarters.

Bombshell faces the groggy Dinobots and says, "Hear me. From now on you will think of the Autobots as your mortal enemies. Your mission is to destroy them and their pathetic earth friends. Now—*transform!*"

Swoop watches his friends turn into their dinosaur forms. The Dinobot rebellion has begun.

Turn to page 5.

The Dinobots are powerful Transformers. In robot form they are mighty warriors. When they transform into giant dinosaurs they are almost unstoppable.

The Dinobots Grimlock, Slag, Sludge, Snarl, and Swoop are feeling disagreeable today. They are bored as they sit by a river that runs through Hidden Valley. The Autobot leader Optimus Prime has asked them to keep a lookout there for approaching Decepticons.

With a flick of his energo-sword, Grimlock flips a stone into the river.

Sludge grunts. "Me bored. No action." Sludge kicks a rock into the river and splashes Slag.

"Hey, Slag wet!" yells the irritable Slag. "That make Slag mad!" He gives Sludge a shove, which Sludge returns. The two Dinobots start to fight.

While the Dinobots argue, push, and shove, they neglect their lookout duties. That is too bad because they miss the sight of the evil Insecticons Bombshell and Kickback approaching from the north.

Stealthily the Insecticons slip behind a stand of fir trees a hundred feet from the riverbank. Suddenly a ball of fire lights the sky as Bombshell shoots a mortar at the squabbling Dinobots.

Turn to page 2.

1

Bumblebee glances back and sees the Decepticons Soundwave and Frenzy behind him. Of course! Soundwave must have picked up the radio transmittal. His sensors can pick up even the weakest radio transmissions.

Bumblebee plunges into the water, hoping to make his escape. A high-pitched shriek from Frenzy stops him cold. Frenzy can produce such a high, grating sound that it disorients his enemies and disrupts the electrical flow of their circuitry, causing them to malfunction. Bumblebee's circuits are hopelessly scrambled and he can't move.

"I think we should leave him right there," says Frenzy. "He'll be a rusty warning to anyone else who tries to spy on us."

Back in the mini-sub, Skids is getting worried. When Bumblebee doesn't come back, he knows something awful must have happened to him. Where on earth is Sludge? Skids wonders, looking directly at the sleeping Dinobot. Should he attempt a rescue on his own? Or should he return to the Ark for help? He's afraid to radio a message, knowing that the Decepticons are nearby and might intercept it.

If you think Skids should return to the Ark for help, turn to page 57.

If you think he should try to rescue Bumblebee on his own, turn to page 68.

4

Optimus Prime decides that Bumblebee and Skids would handle this mission better on their own. Bumblebee and Skids are clearly relieved at his decision as they transform themselves into their car forms and head out.

A red compact and a yellow mini-car drive away from the Ark and travel along a coastal road carved into the mountains. Skids and Bumblebee are heading for Dolphin's Bay, where the mysterious electromagnetic activity was detected. Skids begins to daydream as he gazes at the sparkling water and rugged cliffs all around him. DANGER: HAIRPIN TURN says a wooden sign.

Crash!!! Skids' hood folds in two as he rams into a tree at the edge of the hillside. Bumblebee screeches to a halt and pulls up beside him, transforming to his robot form. "One of these days your daydreaming will get us both killed!" he scolds.

"Never mind that now," Skids says excitedly. "Just look at my detector—it's going wild. The electromagnetic waves are exactly like the ones I picked up off the coast. This must be Mount Lomas, which rises directly above Dolphin's Bay."

Turn to page 18.

Bombshell is beside himself with delight. This is wonderful, he thinks. If the Dinobots can cause lots of trouble, then we can get on with the rest of our plan. This is only the first step! Every thought that Bombshell thinks is transferred into the minds of the Dinobots, but Bombshell doesn't care what they know—he is their master now.

Swoop must stop his friends before they attack the Autobots and the humans.

Even with his bad wing, Swoop can move faster than the other Dinobots. Should he fly to Optimus Prime at Autobot headquarters and warn him that the Dinobots are under Insecticon control? But by then the Dinobots will have already done a lot of damage. Perhaps he should try to fight Bombshell and force him to release the Dinobots.

....
If you think Swoop should fly back to Optimus Prime at Autobot headquarters, turn to page 10.

If you think Swoop should stay and fight Bombshell, turn to page 12.

5

As the Dinobots continue their rampage through Hidden Valley toward the Ark, Swoop is horrified. Trees are knocked over. There are huge holes in the ground.

Swoop catches up with these marauding giants as they approach a farm. He feels helpless as he watches Sludge whack a silo with his tail. The top of the silo flies through the air and smashes into the top of a barn.

Swoop is getting tired. His tiny wings will never carry him to the Ark in time to warn the Autobots. He doesn't know what to do.

Suddenly Swoop feels weird. His whole body tingles. In seconds he is back to normal size. Bombshell's poison has worn off and Swoop zooms off to the Ark.

Turn to page 10.

Prowl looks at the Dinobots who are resting safely back at the Autobot headquarters and he has an idea. "The Decepticons still believe the Dinobots are on their side," he begins. "We could get in touch with Sludge and have him present himself as a friendly scout. He will say the Dinobots have succeeded in their mission and destroyed many Autobot warriors. He will ask Megatron to welcome Grimlock, Slag, Snarl, and Sludge, who are on their way to Mount Lomas.

"In this way, the Dinobots will get behind the Decepticon lines," Prowl explains. "When the rest of our forces arrive, the Dinobots will turn on their unsuspecting hosts and overpower them as we launch our own surprise attack." Prowl concludes his long speech, looking pleased with himself.

"Your plan will take too long. It makes me nervous," Windcharger complains. "Besides, we have to get Bumblebee out of there quickly. Who knows what they'll do to him!"

If you think Optimus Prime should take Prowl's advice, turn to page 11.

If you think he should take Windcharger's advice, turn to page 22.

8

Skids tries to get the emergency systems going, but Frenzy's horrible scream has ruined them. Skids is in a panic. He can't think of any way out of this situation.

The sub does a backflip in the air, then straightens out and heads for a huge gray rock. "This is it!" yells Skids as the rock comes closer and closer. He covers his head and prepares to crash.

The sub hits! But instead of crashing, it bounces back. The rock isn't a rock at all! It's standing up.... It's Sludge! The impact of the crash has left both Sludge and the sub dented, but pretty much unharmed. And the crash has finally stopped the sub.

"Hey, what you doing?" shouts Sludge.

Turn to page 65.

Swoop flies north to Autobot headquarters. Upon landing, he transforms to robot form and bursts into the war room, where he finds Optimus Prime pointing at a map.

"These reports from Hound just don't make any sense," Optimus Prime is saying. "Why would the Dinobots tear up the farmland outside Hidden Valley? They know they are supposed to protect humans—not harm them!"

Finally the Autobot leader notices Swoop. "Do you know what's going on?" he demands as a hush falls over the room.

"Terrible, bad thing happen to Dinobots," Swoop explains. "Bombshell sting the Dinobots. Only me, Swoop, get away. Now Bombshell the Dinobot boss. Me no understand."

Optimus Prime faces the other Autobots squarely. "Bombshell must have stung the Dinobots with his cerebro-shells," he tells them. "Once Bombshell plants a cerebro-shell, he controls his victim's mind. Now that they are under Bombshell's control, the Dinobots are a threat not only to the humans we have pledged to protect, but to ourselves, as well. They must be stopped."

Turn to page 19.

Optimus Prime decides to try Prowl's plan. He calls the Dinobots to the war room and carefully explains the scheme to them. He hopes they have understood.

Swoop leaves the war room and flies to the bay area. He looks for Sludge but he can't find him. He lights down on a huge gray rock. Suddenly the rock begins to move. It's the sleeping Sludge!

Swoop stays on Sludge's huge back. He tries to remember what Optimus Prime told him. "Pretend you still Bombshell's slave," he tells Sludge. "Say Optimus Prime dead. Say other Dinobots coming to be with Megatron. Say him new leader. When you all inside with Decepticons, then we get 'em."

Sludge looks at Swoop blankly. "How me know when to start smashing Decepticons?" Sludge asks.

"Me in sky," Swoop answers. "Me fly a loop. Then you do your thing."

Swoop flies off. The Autobots Seaspray and Topspin are in the channel. Seaspray is in his Destroyer form. He spots Swoop and signals for him to land. Swoop does and transforms on the deck of the giant battleship.

Just as the sun is sinking in the sky, Seaspray cries out, "This is it! Optimus Prime just gave the secret code word to attack!"

Turn to page 40.

Swoop stays and fights. He launches a missile at Bombshell, but misses.

"Oh, so you've managed to escape, have you," sneers Bombshell. The clever Insecticon flies right above the Dinobots and hovers there. "If you fire another missile at me, you'll blast your friends, too," he says.

Swoop is in a tight spot now. Should he fly higher, where the wind is strong? Bombshell will have trouble flying against the wind. But will Swoop's wing, which was injured in the bomb blast, support him in the blustery wind?

Perhaps Swoop should fly below Bombshell. Then he could blast his missile up at Bombshell without hitting his friends.

If you decide Swoop should lure Bombshell higher into the wind, turn to page 70.

If you think Swoop should fly underneath Bombshell and fire up at him, turn to page 35.

12

"Sounds good," says Bumblebee. "That way Skids can go underwater in the sub and help me check out the situation."

Then Sludge steps forward. "Me best water fighter," he brags. "Me go too."

It's true that Sludge might be useful on this mission. But the Dinobots often don't follow orders. Sludge is also slow and slow-witted, as well. Optimus Prime can tell that Skids and Bumblebee would rather go without Sludge.

If you think Optimus Prime should include Sludge in the mission, turn to page 24.

If you think Bumblebee and Skids should go alone, turn to page 3.

Swoop tries desperately to fly away. He hovers above the lizard for a second, but the lizard bats at him and knocks him to the ground.

The lizard is giving every indication that he plans to have Swoop for lunch. "Me very hard to swallow," Swoop tells the lizard as he hops and flaps his wings.

Then suddenly a small breeze comes along and gives Swoop the boost he needs to get him airborne.

Swoop manages to fly away. He flaps his wings furiously as he tries to catch up to the Dinobots. It isn't hard to follow their path. The Dinobots have left a trail of destruction behind them.

Turn to page 6.

Bumblebee and Skids watch from the hut window as Sludge continues his stomping and rocking until he has created a giant tidal wave that pounds against the side of Mount Lomas. He adds to the tumult by whacking his tremendous tail into the water, causing the giant wave to sweep over the mountain.

At last, the side of Mount Lomas slides into the bay. Cries of terror fill the air as Decepticons and lab equipment are all swept out into the bay.

Sludge swims back to the dock when the damage is complete. Bumblebee is back to himself since Sludge swept Frenzy away with his flood. He and Skids meet Sludge on the dock. "Gee," Skids says, laughing, "the Decepticons will never forget the day you *crashed* their party!"

THE END

Just after Sludge nods off, Bumblebee and Skids arrive and start exploring the cove in Wheeljack's mini-submarine. They see a large gray rock in the distance. They don't realize it is the sleeping Sludge.

"That's odd," says Skids, checking his chart. "I don't see a small island marked on the map." But the strange object is quickly forgotten as the sub's instrument panel goes wild.

"That's it! That's the signal I was telling Optimus Prime about!" Skids exclaims.

"Eureka!" yells Bumblebee. "Let's track it to its source."

Skids fiddles with the control knobs on his instrument panel, and a hologram map appears on the screen. "There's no doubt about it—the signals are coming from an underwater tunnel on the coast. And it looks like the tunnel connects to a series of chambers inside Mount Lomas."

The sub draws as close as it can to the coast. "You stay put while I find out what I can about this mysterious underground installation," says Bumblebee. Then he checks his circuits before letting himself out of the hatch.

Turn to page 28.

Bumblebee lifts up a branch to examine Skids' hood and notices a trail hidden in the woods. "This is no nature trail—someone cleared it within the last week," he says to Skids, bending down to look closer. "Look at these footprints—only a giant creature would have feet this big. Or a Decepticon, of course," he adds. "If you can still transform, maybe we should follow it and see if the signals get stronger."

....

If you think Bumblebee and Skids should follow the trail, turn to page 23.

If you think they should continue to Dolphin's Bay to meet the mini-sub, turn to page 25.

18

Optimus Prime turns to Prowl, his logical-minded second-in-command. "I don't want to destroy our friends, Prowl," he says. "Do you have any suggestions?"

"We know that the Dinobots will soon pass through farms and cities and cause even more damage," says the sensible Prowl. "From that point of view, I suggest that a direct and quick attack is our best plan. However, I can consult the memory bank of the Ark's computer to see if it can come up with another plan."

Optimus Prime thinks. He knows that Prowl is right. The Dinobots will cause unbelievable destruction when they arrive at populated areas. Maybe he shouldn't waste precious time with the Ark's computer memory. But the Dinobots have been loyal friends. And there may be information that can save the earth and the Dinobots, too.

If you decide that Optimus Prime should consult the Ark's computer memory banks, turn to page 26.

If you decide the Autobots should destroy the Dinobots immediately by launching a massive attack, turn to page 30.

19

"Our first guests! Welcome," cackles the Constructicon engineer Scrapper, as Skids and Bumblebee hit the ground. Skids is knocked senseless, but Bumblebee straightens himself out and discovers that he is unharmed. He realizes he is in some sort of underground prison.

Bumblebee recognizes Scrapper right away. He is a wizard at designing energy plants for the Decepticons. Bumblebee wonders if his being here is a clue to what is going on. Could the Decepticons be building some sort of underground energy plant? Bumblebee looks around. His cell is in a supermodern underground lab. Through the bars he sees beakers filled with colorful liquids and pots with strange-colored smoke rising out of them.

"Where are we?" he asks Scrapper. "What's going on here?"

"I might as well tell you, since you and your friend aren't going to have the chance to tell anyone else," says Gravedigger. "We have discovered a limitless supply of superfuel that makes us even stronger than before."

Turn to page 39.

Optimus Prime is afraid that Ravage or another spy may have already told the Decepticons that the Dinobots are once again loyal to the Autobot cause. This would mean that Megatron will see through Prowl's clever plan.

So Optimus Prime decides to take Windcharger's advice, and calls his commanders together to plan a direct attack. Powerglide will attack from the air, Seaspray and Topspin will approach Mount Lomas from the bay, and Optimus Prime will lead the main army of warriors in a land attack.

The Autobots arrive in force at the Decepticon stronghold as the sun sinks into the Pacific. Megatron, Starscream, Frenzy, Rumble, and the other Decepticon warriors appear on top of Mount Lomas, outlined against the blood-red sky. Their new energy plant isn't operating yet, but they are supremely confident and eager to fight.

Turn to page 44.

Groaning and clanking, Skids changes into a robot. "Wait for me!" he cries, hurrying after Bumblebee up the trail. With every step they take, the electromagnetic signals get stronger. There's no doubt now that they are close to the source.

"You're interfering with my detector," Skids complains. "Let me go first."

Reluctantly, Bumblebee allows Skids to pass him. A moment later they round a bend in the trail and the ground levels off. Up ahead there is a cave entrance.

"This is it!" Skids shouts, looking at his detector. And he walks rapidly toward the cave.

"*Watch out!*" Bumblebee cries, but the warning comes too late. Skids stumbles over a trip wire, and the ground gives way beneath their feet. Clutching each other in terror, they fall head over heels into the gaping black hole.... They have walked right into a Decepticon trap....

Turn to page 20.

"All right," says Optimus Prime to Sludge, "you can go along on the mission. Just remember that you take your orders from Bumblebee and Skids."

Bumblebee and Skids aren't thrilled to have Sludge along. As cars, they can cover more ground than he can, and they don't want to lose any time. Besides, they think he'll just be in the way.

"We'll meet you in Dolphin's Bay, Sludge," Bumblebee says outside the Ark. When he sees the Dinobot's face fall, he adds, "Don't worry, you won't miss any action. I'm sure we'll be tracking the electromagnetic waves all day."

After Skids and Bumblebee pull away, tires screeching, Sludge sets off for Dolphin's Bay. He makes a wrong turn but he's in luck—it turns out to be a shortcut and Sludge is the first to arrive at Dolphin's Bay.

Sludge stands offshore, waiting. Then he decides to take a nap. Curling his long neck and tail out of sight, he looks exactly like a huge gray rock.

Turn to page 17.

Bumblebee and Skids continue driving down to Dolphin's Bay, where the mini-sub awaits them at the dock. They cast off, sinking deeper in the water as they cruise north along the coast. Bumblebee checks the instrument panel as they pass alongside a black coral reef. The needles go wild. "We're right on top of whatever is causing these crazy electromagnetic waves," he says.

Skids' face lights up. "Maybe this black coral has something to do with the disturbances. I have a hunch," he says, sitting down at the computer in the mini-sub. Skids begins to punch several codes into the computer.

"What are you doing?" asks Bumblebee.

Turn to page 42.

Optimus Prime, Prowl, Windcharger, Mirage, and Swoop form a semicircle around the computer memory bank. Precious minutes go by as the huge computer whirs and clicks. Finally, a message appears on the screen:

A MAGNETIC PULL WILL DISLODGE CEREBRO-SHELLS. WINDCHARGER IS THE AUTOBOT BEST EQUIPPED FOR THIS TASK. THERE IS DANGER! A MAGNETIC FORCE TOO POWERFUL COULD PULL DINOBOTS APART, SHATTERING COMPONENTS. EXACT FORCE REQUIRED IS UNKNOWN AT THIS TIME.

"Can you do it?" Prowl asks Windcharger.

Windcharger is not sure. He doesn't know how close he will have to stand. If he stands too far away, his magnetic field might not be strong enough to pull out the cerebro-shells. Yet, if he stands too close, his magnetic field might cause the Dinobots to be pulled apart when they come in contact with it. It will be a risky business.

Prowl urges Optimus Prime to make a quick decision. "According to my calculations," he says, "the Dinobots are approaching Bandit's Bluff. That means they will reach the nearest city in fifteen minutes. We don't have a second to lose!"

Go on to page 27.

"I have another idea," suggests Mirage. "I could use my electro-disrupter to cast a mirage at the edge of Bandit's Bluff, which overlooks the ocean."

"What good would that do?" asks Jazz.

"Well," Mirage continues thoughtfully, "I can create an image of Optimus Prime standing on the bluff. When the Dinobots see him, they will think it's really Optimus Prime and they'll attack. They will run right through the image and fall into the ocean."

"Excellent," says Prowl. "The water and the fall will knock them out without really hurting them. Then it will be a simple matter to capture them and have Windcharger remove the cerebro-shells safely back at the Ark."

"I don't know," murmurs Windcharger. "I think it would be better if I used my magnetic field."

If you think Optimus Prime should let Mirage create an illusion, turn to page 45.

If you think he should let Windcharger use his magnetism to remove the cerebro-shells, turn to page 66.

Bumblebee swims into the tunnel. Before long, the tunnel slants upward and he finds himself only waist-deep in water. Up ahead he sees a doorway which must lead to the chamber inside.

Bumblebee steps warily up to the doorway. He thinks he recognizes the voice of Megatron on the other side: "In just a few short hours, we will vanquish our enemies. The energy plant will be finished by nightfall. And with the superfuel processed from black coral growing underwater at our very door, we will be utterly invincible."

The Decepticons yell and cheer as Bumblebee sneaks off. He wants to return to the sub, but he knows every second counts and radios ahead to Skids.

"*Don't move!*" a deep voice booms. "The game is over!"

Turn to page 4.

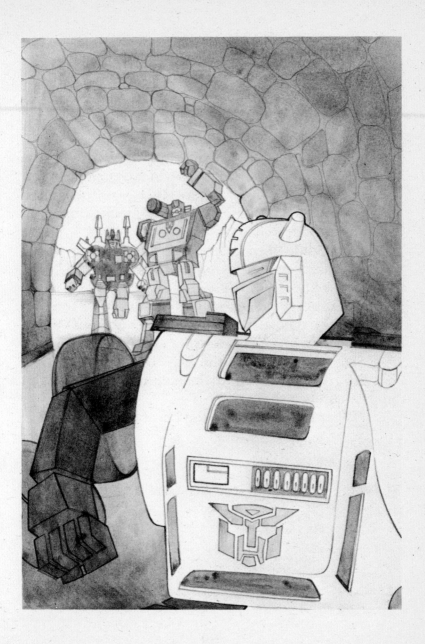

There isn't a moment to lose, so Optimus Prime and the Autobots launch a full-scale attack on the Dinobots.

They encounter the mighty creatures, who are approaching a big city.

"Attack now," orders Optimus Prime.

"Hate to do this, old buddy," says Tracks as he fires his blinding black-beam gun into Grimlock's eyes. The fearsome Dinobot rears back, confused and blinded by the beam. He charges in Tracks' direction, but he can't see.

Powerglide flies in close and drops one of his small concussion bombs on Snarl. *Roarrrrr!!!* Snarl falls to his knees.

The enraged Slag sends a jet of fire from his mouth toward Powerglide. Swoop flies in from behind him and fires one of his missiles at the giant Dinobot.

Slag staggers from the blast of Swoop's missile, hits the ground with an earth-shaking thud . . . and out pops a cerebro-shell!

"What happen?" asks the bewildered Slag.

Turn to page 72.

Skids can't stand this crazy roller-coaster ride another second. He fires his electron blaster at the control panel. The blast stops the sub all right, but it also blows out the glass window next to the console.

The rush of water knocks Skids against the wall. His circuits fizzle and short out. He slumps over, and the sub, now filled with water, sinks to the bottom of the bay.

Turn to page 67.

Barooooom!!! The huge slab of metal lands on the edge of the bluff with a tremendous thud. In seconds the Autobots are shielding themselves from fragments of metal that are flying through the air. Then it becomes very quiet. When the Autobots dare to look, they see Grimlock, Slag, Snarl, and Sludge in pieces strewn across the ground.

Prowl walks over and picks up three small pieces of metal. "So these are cerebro-shells," he says sadly. "I will have to study them."

Windcharger sighs. "My magnetism was too much for them. I didn't want this to happen."

But it has happened. Except for Swoop, the once mighty Dinobots have met the same fate as the original dinosaurs—they are now extinct!

THE END

Skids and Bumblebee hurry back to the Ark to tell Optimus Prime about Operation Black Coral. "We've analyzed the data on the Ark's computer," says Skids. "The plant must be underground, deep inside Mount Lomas, which overlooks Dolphin's Bay."

"Then we must destroy that plant," says Optimus Prime. The Autobots follow Optimus Prime into the war room, where he maps out a strategy for seizing Mount Lomas from the Decepticons.

An hour later a long convoy of vehicles travels at breakneck speed toward Dolphin's Bay. Decepticon spy jets overhead see them approaching and report back to Megatron.

Megatron and his Decepticon army are waiting for the Autobots when they arrive at Mount Lomas. Megatron shouts a strange challenge to Optimus Prime. "I challenge you, and you alone, to fight to the end!" he cries.

"It's a trick," says Prowl.

"Don't do it," advises Sunstreaker.

But Optimus Prime wants to save the lives of his Autobots if he can. "I accept your challenge," he calls to Megatron. "Let the battle begin!"

Turn to page 62.

Ten minutes later the destroyer rounds Sea Lion Point at the southern end of the cove. "Looks like we've made it!" says Bumblebee.

"I'm not so sure, guys," Seaspray says as a fighter plane streaks across the sky. "Starscream is after us ...but I won't give up without a fight!"

But Seaspray only has a chance to fire one laser before an ominous buzz fills the air.

Baaaaroooom! Starscream's cluster bombs make a direct hit on the sleek destroyer, shattering it to bits. In only minutes the hull fills with water and the big ship goes down. It looks like there's no stopping Operation Black Coral now.

This time the Autobots are truly sunk!

THE END

Swoop flies underneath Bombshell and gets ready to shoot at him. Swoop could fly directly over Slag. That's where his best shot would be. But Slag has a nasty temper and shoots red-hot flames into the air when he is angry.

Swoop could also try to fire at Bombshell from above Sludge. This would be a much tougher shot, but Sludge is less likely to attack him.

Swoop has to make his move now or Bombshell will leave and the Dinobots will be in his power forever.

....

If you think Swoop should risk flying above Slag, turn to page 36.

If you decide he should play it safe and fly above Sludge, turn to page 48.

Swoop flies above Slag. Slag begins to get up just as Swoop flies over his head.

"Blast him!" Bombshell screams to the Dinobots.

But before they can, Swoop drops his missile. It's a direct hit. The tiny Insecticon spirals to the ground.

Slag jumps out of the way of the falling Insecticon. He, Sludge, Snarl, and Grimlock are on their feet, but they look curiously blank. Since Bombshell is out cold, he can't control the Dinobots. This is Swoop's chance to force Bombshell to free his friends.

Swoop lands and transforms into his robot form. He holds Bombshell tightly in his hand and shakes him.

"Wake up, ugly bug, or Swoop crush," he shouts.

Slowly Bombshell comes to.

"Me give you order," says Swoop. "Make my friends better...or me flatten you."

Bombshell is afraid and he obeys Swoop. Then he flies away as fast as he can.

Turn to page 56.

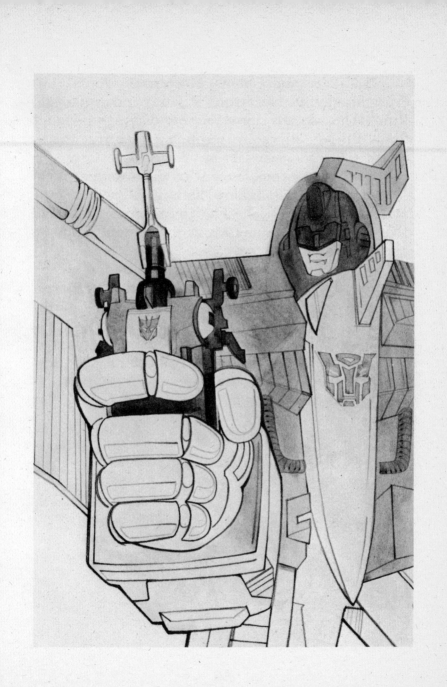

"Rumble, no!" shouts Megatron. "You'll ruin everything!" But Megatron's warning comes too late. Rumble has already started a groundwave to stop Optimus Prime's attack. In seconds a powerful earthquake splits the mountain in two.

The Decepticons know what the Autobots don't —the mountain is hollow because it contains the Decepticons' secret lab. The Decepticons panic and flee down the mountainside as the ground crumbles beneath their feet.

The Autobots, too, run down the mountain. They make it to the bottom in time to see the Decepticon lab buried beneath the rubble of Rumble's earthquake.

"So much for Operation Black Coral," Skids says, laughing. He's right. Operation Black Coral gets a new name in the Decepticon computer file—Operation Earthquake Mistake.

THE END

Scrapper consults his blueprints, then looks at Bumblebee with an evil smile. "In order to finish the energy plant I designed, I need more materials. It's nice of you to oblige."

Laughing with glee, the Constructicon wastes no time. In less than ten minutes he turns Bumblebee and Skids into scrap metal, which he uses to help finish his energy plant.

One by one all of the Autobots come looking for their missing friends and fall into Scrapper's sinister trap. The Constructicon is able to build an entire plant out of Autobot pieces. He names it "The Autobot Memorial Power Plant" and laughs at how he was able to make the once-powerful Autobots look so *fuelish*!

THE END

Swoop transforms and flies toward shore. It looks like the Decepticons are having a victory celebration on top of Mount Lomas. Grimlock, Slag, Snarl, and Sludge stand with a dozen Decepticons around a blazing bonfire. Megatron stands apart, addressing his troops.

Grimlock looks up and sees Swoop approaching in the distance. Optimus Prime told him that when Swoop makes a loop-the-loop flight pattern in the sky, it is the signal for the Dinobots to attack the Decepticons.

Grimlock sees Swoop fly in the loop pattern. "What he mean?" he says. "Oh, yes! Me remember."

"Attack!" shouts Grimlock to the other Dinobots.

Turn to page 64.

"Are you all right?" he asks when Bumblebee is safely inside with the sack of black coral he found.

"I'll admit that explosion shook me up a little, but luckily I wasn't hurt. How on earth did you get those dolphins to get me out of the canyon?" Bumblebee asks.

"There'll be time to explain later," Skids answers as he sits down to start the sub. "Right now we've got to get back to the Ark."

When they reach the dock, Skids taps out a message of thanks to the dolphins. As the yellow mini-car and the red compact speed away, they see a dozen dolphins leap out of the water, as if to say good-bye.

Turn to page 33.

"I'm trying to break into the Decepticon computer," Skids answers. "It may not get us anywhere, but I was thinking that *if* this black coral does have something to do with the disturbances, and *if* the Decepticons are behind it, then the Decepticon computer might have a file on it. We just have to break into that computer file."

"How do we do that?"

"We try to think of a code word," says Skids.

"Try *Black Coral*," suggests Bumblebee.

No sooner does Skids type in the words BLACK CORAL than the screen of the computer lights up with the words:

ENERGY POTENTIAL OF BLACK CORAL IS UNLIMITED. CONSTRUCTICONS HAVE DEVELOPED CONVERSION PROCESS. SUPERFUEL CAN BE MADE FROM BLACK CORAL. SUPERFUEL WILL TRIPLE CURRENT WAR CAPABILITIES. STRATEGIC ADVANTAGE OVER ENEMIES. ADVISE IMMEDIATE PLANNING SESSION ON OPERATION BLACK CORAL TO...

Turn to page 60.

Megatron spies Topspin and Seaspray approaching from atop Mount Lomas. He orders his warrior jets to attack them.

The Decepticon Skywarp drops a heat-seeking missile on Topspin. The Autobot can't get out of the way fast enough. *Boom!!!*

"Hey, you can't do that to my pal!" yells Seaspray, shooting his lasers at the jets. Seaspray gets help when Powerglide and Tracks fly into view.

"Take this, you buzzards!" yells Powerglide, blasting the Decepticon jets with his thermal beam.

"Got him," cheers Tracks.

Optimus Prime and his army approach from land. The Autobots storm the entrance to Mount Lomas. Once inside, Jazz uses his flamethrower to set fire to the fuel-producing equipment while Ratchet rushes into the tunnel and pulls out Bumblebee. "Things will be too hot to handle in a few minutes!" shouts Jazz. "Let's get out of here."

The fire rages within the mountain as Operation Black Coral becomes Operation Black Ashes. The Autobots have won!

THE END

Optimus Prime decides to go ahead with Mirage's plan. The Autobots travel at top speed toward the ocean and Bandit's Bluff. Mirage casts an illusion at the end of the bluff. First a ghostly outline of Optimus Prime takes shape. Then the details of the Autobot leader are filled in.

When Sludge appears in the distance, he is sure he sees Optimus Prime standing on the edge of the bluff, fully armed and gleaming in the sunlight.

The other Dinobots are faster and they outdistance Sludge as they charge toward the image of Optimus Prime.

"Dinobots kill Autobots...Dinobots kill...." The Dinobots chant this over and over as they charge toward the bluff.

The Autobots watch from behind some rocks in the distance. "I don't know about this plan," whispers Prowl doubtfully.

"It will work," says Mirage uneasily.

Turn to page 71.

45

Skids sits down at the console and asks the computer to analyze the clicks and high-pitched whistles coming from the dolphins. Five minutes later the powerful computer has figured out one hundred basic words.

"I only hope this works," Skids mutters as he turns the sonar equipment to its highest frequency and taps out a greeting.

The dolphins stop what they are doing and turn attentively toward the sub. Quickly, Skids asks them to go get Bumblebee. The intelligent creatures seem to understand and swim over to the top of the canyon where Bumblebee disappeared. The three largest dolphins push aside the coral pillars that are trapping him.

Skids breathes a sigh of relief a moment later when he sees Bumblebee swimming toward him. Eagerly, Skids helps his friend into the sub.

Turn to page 41.

Swoop positions himself above Sludge. He can barely see Bombshell, but he fires anyway and manages to hit his target. It's a lucky shot.

"*Eeeeeeeek!!!*" Bombshell shrieks, and flutters to the ground.

Now Swoop transforms to robot mode and holds his thermal sword above Bombshell.

"Set Dinobots free," he threatens. "Or Bombshell in big trouble."

Bombshell knows when it's time to give up. "I'll do anything you want, but please let me live!" he begs. Then he removes the cerebro-shells from the Dinobots' heads.

"Bombshell go now, or Swoop squash!" yells Swoop.

As Bombshell transforms into robot form and limps away, the Dinobots return to their normal selves. Slag and Sludge start fighting again, and accidentally clobber Swoop on the head. Swoop feels himself getting dizzy...then everything turns black.

Turn to page 58.

Skids heads for the channel, steering his sub through the giant kelp forest. He knows the Decepticons must be in the area, and he hopes the kelp will hide him.

Finally he arrives at the channel. He taps out a message to Seaspray: S...O...S. Seaspray gets the message and transforms into his destroyer form so he can rush to Dolphin's Bay. He sees Skids' mini-sub surface when he arrives.

Skids climbs aboard the destroyer and explains what has happened. Together they return to the coral canyon that has Bumblebee trapped within it. Seaspray carefully uses his laser to cut away the coral. When he has cleared a large enough space, Bumblebee squeezes through and swims to the surface.

"Thank goodness you're all right," says Skids, helping Bumblebee aboard the destroyer.

"It was more trouble than I expected, but I got it," says Bumblebee, presenting Skids with a chunk of black coral.

"Now all we have to do is get out of here alive," says Skids. "I think our best bet is to stay with Seaspray. His sonar will tell us if there are any more underwater mines around here. He can take us back to the Ark."

Turn to page 34.

Windcharger stands about 100 feet from the stampeding Dinobots and transmits a magnetic field.

Pop...pop...pop...pop...as Grimlock, Slag, Snarl, and Sludge lumber by, the four cerebro-shells fall to the ground. Suddenly the Dinobots stop short. They look confused.

Prowl steps forward. "How do you feel?" he asks.

"No good," Grimlock confesses.

"Who are your friends?" Prowl asks, testing.

"Slag, Sludge, Snarl, Swoop," answers Grimlock.

"And what about the Autobots?" asks Prowl.

Grimlock hesitates a moment. "Autobots good... Autobots friends." The dumbfounded Dinobots watch as the Autobots cheer and clap.

Back at the Autobot headquarters that night, Optimus Prime congratulates Windcharger on the success of his plan. There is a big celebration welcoming the Dinobots back.

All the Dinobots are in good spirits, except for Grimlock. "Grimlock try to remember," he tells Huffer, "but no can remember. Thing important, but no can remember."

"Is it something Bombshell said?" Huffer coaches.

"That it! Grimlock remember now!" shouts the huge Dinobot. "Must tell." He runs clumsily to Optimus Prime.

Turn to page 59.

"You stay," says Sludge, lifting Skids onto the dock.

"What are you up to?" asks Skids.

"You see," Sludge answers. "Sludge make big wave."

Skids hides in a nearby hut, and watches as Sludge moves out into the water near where Bumblebee was last seen. He begins rocking from foot to foot, creating tremendous waves around him. Soon Sludge is stomping down one foot, then the other. The water above and below is turbulent.

The force of the churning water carries Bumblebee out of the tunnel. Freed from his captivity in the tunnel, but still unable to move, Bumblebee floats to the surface. Sludge grabs him in his great jaws and carries him to the dock. There he sets him down. Skids runs out of the hut and drags Bumblebee inside. "Thank goodness!" cries Skids.

Turn to page 16.

Skids is getting sick. He could try to short-circuit the sub by using his own electron blaster. If this plan works, all the circuits will be blown and the sub will simply stop. But if the blast is too strong, it's hard to say what will happen.

He could also try to activate the emergency power supply and steering. If he gets the backup systems working, he might be able to regain control of the mini-sub.

If you think Skids should use his electron blaster to short-circuit the sub, turn to page 31.

If you think Skids should try to activate the sub's emergency systems, turn to page 9.

52

Kabooom!! "Oh, no!" Bumblebee gasps when he feels the explosion—the coral was booby-trapped. Tossed up and down by churning water, Bumblebee is helpless when the shockwave hits. He struggles to break free, but he's caught in a whirlpool that sucks him down, along with huge pieces of broken coral.

When the water clears, Skids can't see Bumblebee anywhere. The dolphins, frightened by the noise, have also disappeared. Skids drives the sub over to the reef and sees that Bumblebee has been trapped in a deep coral canyon.

Skids can't leave the cabin without underwater gear, so he can't clear away the coral pillars that are trapping his friend.

Skids could head for the channel, where he might be able to radio Seaspray for help. But the channel is five miles away and Skids doesn't know if Bumblebee is hurt, or what might happen if he leaves him all alone.

Turn to page 61.

Windcharger decides he has to stop the Dinobots—at all costs. As they clunk by, he stands forty feet away and releases a powerful magnetic field.

The Dinobots stop dead in their tracks, as if they've run into a steel wall. They look stunned. Then suddenly they jerk into motion. Grimlock rears up, snapping his jaws while Sludge whacks the ground with his tail. Meanwhile Slag runs in a circle around them, shooting fire. Snarl starts flapping his spinal plates and pawing the ground like a bull.

"The magnetism is too much—they'll be ripped apart!" shouts Prowl as bolts, screws, and bits of metal fly away from the whirling Dinobots. "I'm afraid you're right," Windcharger replies with a frown, "but there's nothing we can do."

The Dinobots speed up, repeating the same movements again and again like crazed wind-up toys. Faster and faster they go as arms and legs start to fly through the air. "Watch out!" yells Prowl. "Here comes Sludge's tail!"

Turn to page 32.

Slowly the Dinobots return to their old selves, but they are really confused! "Slag feel funny," says the huge Dinobot.

"Grimlock, too," says Grimlock.

"What happen?" asks Snarl.

"You no worry," Swoop says with a laugh. "You just have bug in circuits."

THE END

Skids surfaces in the sub and gets out. He steps onto the dock and transforms himself into his car form. The red car speeds along the coast road, then screeches to a halt in front of the Ark. Skids strides into the war room where Optimus Prime, Windcharger, and Prowl await news of his mission.

In a rush of words Skids tells them of Bumblebee's disappearance and the terrible news about Operation Black Coral.

Windcharger leaps to his feet. "What are we waiting for? Let's attack by land and sea before they finish producing their superfuel. It's our only chance."

Prowl disagrees. "Not so fast, my rash friend. A mountain fortress is almost impossible to storm. In short, we won't stand a chance in a head-on attack. I think we must rely on a clever plan, rather than brute force."

"What exactly do you have in mind, Prowl?" demands Optimus Prime.

Turn to page 8.

Five minutes later, he opens his eyes to find Snarl, Slag, Sludge, and Grimlock standing over him.

"Ha!" Grimlock laughs. "Swoop fall down. Grimlock just give little hit."

"Swoop okay," Swoop says, rubbing his head. Swoop knows something just happened, but he doesn't know what. The hit on the head made him forget Bombshell and the cerebro-shells.

Now you're the only one who knows what really happened!

THE END

"Grimlock have news," Grimlock tells Optimus Prime. "Bombshell say attacking Dinobots only part of plan. Bombshell say Decepticons have bigger plan."

"That certainly is important," says Optimus Prime. He thinks for a minute, and then he turns to Skids. "Could the Decepticons' plan have something to do with that strange electromagnetic activity by Dolphin's Bay you were just telling me about?" he asks.

"It is possible," answers Skids. "Remember that we spotted Decepticons in that area only a week ago."

"Why don't you go down to the bay and scout around, Skids," suggests Optimus Prime. "Take Bumblebee with you. He can explore underwater."

Wheeljack, the mechanical engineer, looks up when he hears the word *underwater*. "This would be a good chance to test out the new mini-submarine that I've been building," he suggests. "I can program it by remote control to meet you at the bay."

Turn to page 13.

"Whoops," says Skids as the screen goes blank. "I guess they figured out that we broke into their computer. Let's get back to headquarters fast! I'm not exactly sure what the Decepticons are up to, but if they've discovered a superfuel, it can't be good!"

"We can't leave until we get a sample of that mysterious black coral," Bumblebee says, letting himself out of the hatch.

Bumblebee leaves Skids in the sub and swims around towering pillars of crimson coral, then through a forest of giant kelp. In front of the black coral he is approached by a school of dolphins, which circles around him, trying to play. Bumblebee is delighted and wishes he could stay awhile, but he knows his mission is more important. So he gives the boldest dolphin a friendly pat and swims past him to the reef. As he breaks off a chunk of black coral...

....

Turn to page 53.

Skids frowns in concentration, trying to think of a way to help Bumblebee.

One by one he sees the dolphins return, gliding gracefully through the giant kelp near the black coral reef. The boldest dolphin swims over to the window of the mini-sub and peers in. He even knocks on the glass with his nose. Looking out the window, Skids sees that the leader is swimming through the coral pillars that have fallen over the canyon where Bumblebee is trapped.

All of a sudden, Skids' face lights up as he gets an idea. Using the sub's computer, he might be able to decode the dolphins' language and ask them to rescue Bumblebee.

It's a long shot. Maybe it would be safer to head for the channel and try to radio the Autobot destroyer Seaspray. But by then it could be too late!

....

If you think Skids should decode the dolphins' language and ask for help, turn to page 46.

If you think Skids should head for the channel to radio Seaspray, turn to page 49.

61

In a few strides Optimus Prime has joined Megatron on the top of Mount Lomas. The two powerful leaders circle each other warily, each waiting for the other to make the first move. Their warriors stand at respectful distances around them.

Finally Megatron fires his nuclear fusion cannon, but Optimus Prime evades the blast by splitting into three units: Optimus, the brain center, armed with a laser rifle; Roller, the spy; and Combat Deck, a fully armed artillery robot.

Optimus Prime has taken Megatron by surprise and the Decepticon leader finds himself outgunned.

Impulsively Rumble jumps forward to help Megatron. Shouting "Death to all Autobots!" he begins pounding the ground with his powerful earthquake-making arms.

Turn to page 38.

Suddenly the Dinobots transform into their dinosaur forms. Before the Decepticons have time to react, the Dinobots strike.

Sludge stomps on the nearby Soundwave. Grimlock charges the evil Frenzy, breaking him in two.

Starscream fires his laser at Slag. The laser bounces off Slag's armor plates and hits Starscream's gun, melting it.

Thrust transforms into a jet and takes to the sky. But Swoop is ready for him. He fires a missile and sends Thrust plummeting to the ground.

Snarl cocks back his tail and hits Megatron, just as Megatron is about to fire his nuclear fusion cannon up at Swoop. Instead of hitting Swoop, Megatron blasts a huge hole in the side of Mount Lomas.

A platoon of Autobots soon arrives to help the Dinobots. They make their way into the hole Megatron has blasted and run down the steps into the underground laboratory. In minutes they free Bumblebee and destroy the fuel-producing equipment. Everything goes according to plan.

That night the Autobots throw a victory party. The Dinobots are unusually merry. Nothing cheers up a Dinobot like a day of fighting Decepticons.

THE END

Skids looks out the hatch of the sub—which is now bobbing up and down near Sludge. "Sludge," he scolds. "Where have you been?"

"Sludge wait for you," Sludge answers irritably. "Where you been?"

"Never mind that now," Skids says, climbing onto Sludge's huge back. "Take me to the dock and I'll try to explain it all to you."

On the way to shore Skids tells Sludge about the energy plant inside Mount Lomas and about the underwater tunnel that leads to it.

"Bumblebee must be trapped in there," says Skids. "We must get him out."

"Yes," agrees Sludge.

"We also have to stop Operation Black Coral while we still can," Skids tells him. "If the Decepticon computer was telling the truth, it won't be long before the Decepticons are super robots."

Turn to page 51.

"All right, Windcharger," says Optimus Prime, "you can try your plan. I'll stay here at the Ark to confer with Skids. He has some urgent business to discuss."

Windcharger roars up the winding road to the bluff, a red sportscar leading a small convoy of cars. They arrive on the windy bluff just as the Dinobots appear in the distance.

Windcharger has to decide where to stand as the Dinobots pass by. He knows his magnetism will be strong enough if he stands forty feet from the Dinobots' path. If he stands farther back, he's less likely to hurt the Dinobots, but he's also not sure if his magnetism will be able to pull out the cerebro-shells.

If you think Windcharger should stand forty feet from the Dinobots, turn to page 54.

If you think he should stand farther back, turn to page 50.

66

This could be the end for Skids...but it's not! With a *whoosh*! the small sub is lifted out of the water. It is held gently in the giant jaws of Sludge!

Sludge carries the sub to the deck of Seaspray, who is in his destroyer form. He was sent to see what the matter was when radio communication between the sub and Autobot headquarters was cut off. With him is Ratchet. Ratchet pulls Skids out of the sub and goes to work repairing his circuits.

When Skids comes to, he tells them of Operation Black Coral. "We have to get Bumblebee and destroy that power plant—while we still can," he urges them.

The Autobots radio headquarters. Optimus Prime launches a full-scale attack. First Skids and Ratchet go in after Bumblebee in the repaired sub. Before the Decepticons can attack them, they pull Bumblebee aboard while the other Autobots direct a hail of firepower on the seaward wall of Mount Lomas. The mountainside crumbles into the sea, causing the water from the bay to crash into the Decepticons' secret lab.

Good thing you decided to have Sludge along on this mission. Since he was there to save Skids, Operation Black Coral is now a total washout.

THE END

Skids steers the sub closer to the tunnel. He must try to rescue Bumblebee. Skids decides to take a risk, and sends out the weakest radio transmission he can. If Bumblebee is closer than the Decepticons, perhaps he will pick up the message before the Decepticons do.

"Do you read me, Bumblebee?...Do you read me?"

Suddenly the radio goes dead and the lights on the control console black out. At the same time, a high-pitched squeal makes Skids cringe. "Oh, no! Frenzy!" he moans, recognizing the maddening sound. The signal is coming from far enough away that Skids doesn't short-circuit, but the sound is causing the mini-sub to run wild.

Skids holds on for dear life as the sub speeds crazily through the water. Its circuits are scrambled and the sub is out of control. It shoots up like a cannonball, breaking through the surface waves, then loops back down at top speed. The sub zigzags through the water, barely missing several boulders.

Turn to page 52.

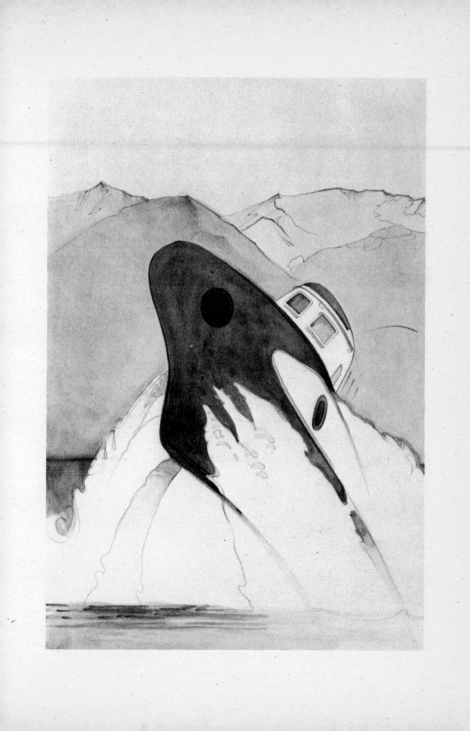

Swoop struggles to fly higher. But instead of following him, Bombshell shouts, "Grimlock, Slag, Snarl, Sludge . . . I command you to attack the Autobot headquarters. Trample any human settlements you pass along the way. Give the earthlings a taste of the terror to come!"

The Dinobots thunder across the valley, raising a cloud of dust as they go. Swoop is blinded by the dust, and Bombshell sees his chance to attack. The huge, ungainly bird feels a prick beneath one wing as Bombshell jabs him with his stinger and flies away.

Swoop glides to the ground. He feels very strange. Although he doesn't notice it, his shadow is growing smaller and smaller. That's because he is shrinking! In seconds he's as small as a hummingbird!

Swoop hops along the ground trying to fly, but he's not used to having such tiny wings. How will he warn the Autobots that the Dinobots are on the rampage? The Autobots will be in big trouble.

Suddenly Swoop is in big trouble himself. A lizard has spotted Swoop and he's coming over to get a closer look.

Turn to page 15.

Mirage's plan does work. Once the Dinobots realize that Optimus Prime is not real, it's too late. With a deafening roar they topple over the edge of the bluff and crash into the ocean.

At the shore below wait the destroyer Seaspray, the repair expert Ratchet, and Sunstreaker, Huffer, Sideswipe, and Bumblebee. They push and pull, using ropes and chains, until they have secured the unconscious Dinobots aboard Seaspray. They head back to the Ark, where Windcharger is waiting to pull out the cerebro-shells. By doing it in the Autobot laboratory, Windcharger has no doubt that he can control his magnetism, and there will be no risk to the Dinobots.

As the destroyer turns the point of Bandit's Bluff, Ratchet laughs as he dries off the soaking Dinobots. "This was one Decepticon plan that was all wet!" he chuckles.

THE END

Optimus Prime now realizes what he has to do. "Bring them down fast and hard," he orders.

"This is for your own good," says Warpath as he aims a volley of his explosive sonic shells at Sludge. Sludge hits the ground with a tremendous smash. Out comes his cerebro-shell.

The next to fall is Snarl. Swoop blasts him with a missile from above. Snarl swings his tail wildly and then falls to his side, banging his head on the ground. His cerebro-shell rolls out.

"Okay, tough guy, you're coming down too!" yells Sideswipe as he blasts Grimlock. But Grimlock won't go down. "Hey, some help over here," calls Sideswipe to Sunstreaker.

"Here we go," Sunstreaker answers, firing a series of high-energy electron pulses. Finally Grimlock hits the ground with a smash, and out falls the final cerebro-shell.

When the Dinobots come to, the Autobots explain what happened.

"Grimlock think Autobots enjoy," snarls Grimlock.

"Autobots hit Snarl. Snarl mad," sulks Snarl.

The Autobots just laugh. The Dinobots are definitely themselves again.

THE END